This book belongs to:

_____

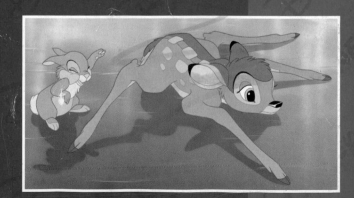

Ursula

Flounder

Triton

STARRING

Ariel

Sebastian

This edition published by
Parragon in 2007

Parragon
Queen Street House
4 Queen Street
Bath, BA1 1HE, UK

ISBN 978-1-4054-7086-5
Printed in China

Disney's THE LITTLE MERMAID

p

Down in the deepest ocean, there once lived a mermaid princess called Ariel. She was the youngest daughter of King Triton, ruler of the merpeople, and she had the most beautiful singing voice in the whole of his kingdom. Her father loved her dearly, but she was always getting into trouble.

Ariel longed to be part of the human world and spent her time exploring old shipwrecks.

The Sea-King feared for
her safety and, thinking
humans were dangerous,
warned her to stay away
from them. But the little
mermaid was certain he
was wrong.

When Ariel was sixteen years old, King Triton arranged for her to sing in a magnificent concert, and merpeople came from all over the kingdom to hear her.

That evening Ariel was so busy exploring with her friend Flounder that she forgot all about the concert! She had found some human treasures and taken them to the surface to ask Scuttle the seagull what they were.

King Triton was furious. "You could have been seen by one of those humans!" he raged. "I'm never to hear of you going to the surface again. Is that clear?"

Ariel tried to protest but her father wouldn't listen. He ordered Sebastian, Ariel's music teacher, to keep an eye on her. But it wasn't an easy task!

One day Sebastian followed Ariel and Flounder to the surface to watch a ship! On board the crew were celebrating the birthday of a handsome prince called Eric, and Ariel watched them in delight.

When they were out of sight, Ariel swam home. "Some day," she vowed to herself, "I'm going to be part of that human world."

Sebastian had seen everything, and it was not long before the Sea-King learnt that Ariel was in love with a human. Triton was very angry. Determined to teach his daughter a lesson, he stormed into her secret grotto and destroyed all her beloved human treasures.

Heartbroken, Ariel sat down and wept. Above her, two sly-looking eels called Flotsam and Jetsam emerged from the shadows. The little mermaid looked up.

"Poor sweet child," they hissed. "Don't be scared. We know someone who can make all your dreams come true. Ursula has great powers."

"The Sea-Witch!" gasped Ariel. She knew that Ursula was her father's worst enemy, who had been banished from his kingdom many years ago and who was now seeking revenge.

A scroll appeared in Ursula's hand. "Go ahead and sign,"
she urged.

Ariel was terrified but, thinking of Eric again, she signed.
A moment later she was walking on the seashore –
a human at last.

Prince Eric had been searching everywhere for the girl with the beautiful voice who had rescued him. He had almost given up hope of finding her, when he noticed someone sitting on a rock. This girl looked familiar but, when he found she couldn't speak, Eric realized sadly that she wasn't the one.

to
th

Later, disguised as Vanessa, a beautiful maiden, and with
Ariel's voice trapped in a seashell necklace, Ursula made her
way to the shore, where the Prince was wandering alone.

As soon as Eric heard Ariel's voice he was entranced and fell completely under its spell. He led Vanessa to the palace, and the very next day announced that they were to be married. The wedding ship was to depart at sunset.

Ariel and her friends watched in despair as the sun lowered in the sky.

By chance, Scuttle discovered that Vanessa was really
Ursula in disguise, and he called on all the sea creatures to
stop the wedding. Sebastian went to find the Sea-King, and
Flounder helped Ariel towards the wedding ship.

Suddenly birds swooped down on Vanessa. A lobster
pinched her nose and some seals flipped her into the
wedding cake!

In the chaos, Vanessa's seashell necklace broke and the beautiful voice inside flew back to its rightful owner. Eric, released from the spell, took Ariel in his arms. Just as he was about to kiss her, the sun sank below the horizon.

Straightaway Ariel was turned back into a mermaid. Ursula grabbed her and dived into the water. Her evil cackle echoed eerily around the ship.

"Ursula, stop!" thundered King Triton, rearing up in front of the Sea-Witch. "Let her go!"

"No!" cried Ursula. "She's mine now. You see, we made a deal! However, I might be willing to make an exchange for someone even better," she suggested slyly.

Triton felt he had no choice. He changed the signature on the scroll to his own and handed over his magic trident to the Sea-Witch.

"At last! It's all mine."
Ursula screamed. "I am
the ruler of the ocean!"
Just then a sharp pain
shot through her arm.
It was a harpoon thrown
by Eric. He had come to
rescue Ariel.

The Sea-Witch swelled with
anger and towered above them. She summoned all the
sea's power and stirred up a giant whirlpool, dragging up
ancient shipwrecks from the seabed.